C0053 71938

THE PRINCESS OF HERSELF

ROBERTA ALLEN

D0928868

The Princess of Herself by Roberta Allen

ISBN-10: 1-938349-70-9

ISBN-13: 978-1-938349-70-6

eISBN-13: 978-1-938349-71-3

Library of Congress Control Number: 2017939950

Copyright © 2017 Roberta Allen

This is a work of fiction. Names, characters, places, events and incidents are either the products of the author's imagination or used in a fictitious manner. Any resemblance to actual persons, living or dead, or actual events is purely coincidental.

Layout and book design by Roberta Allen and Mark Givens

Artwork by Roberta Allen

First Pelekinesis printing 2017

For information:

Pelekinesis, 112 Harvard Ave #65, Claremont, CA 91711 USA

www.pelekinesis.com

THE PRINCESS OF HERSELF
Roberta Allen

Books by Roberta Allen

Fiction

The Traveling Woman

The Daughter

Certain People

The Dreaming Girl

The Princess of Herself

Nonfiction

Amazon Dream

Fast Fiction

The Playful Way to Serious Writing

The Playful Way to Knowing Yourself

PRAISE FOR *THE PRINCESS OF HERSELF*

"Roberta Allen's sharp, jarring stories are bitingly honest and funny as hell. These sixty-ish characters grapple with messy pasts, simmering rivalries, and longings both sexual and transcendent. Rarely has anyone written so frankly about aging, and the ways we create our own past."

> —Dawn Raffel, author of *The Secret Life of Objects*"

"*The Princess of Herself* peekaboos narrative until it lands where? You never know. Filtered through a guest who sees it all, the stories, sometimes deliciously vicious, entertain with great sophistication. Great fun, a dazzling wit."

> —Terese Svoboda

PRAISE FOR ROBERTA ALLEN'S PREVIOUS BOOKS

"Her stories intimately convey the spiritual malaise of people at odds with... their own deeply shrouded impulses."

—The New York Times Book Review

"Allen's gift is for showing how things go sour between people unexpectedly."

—Gary Indiana

"Roberta Allen transmits the pain and compensating strangeness of living in vignettes as urgent and enigmatic as telegrams."

—John Ashbery

"In these short, often poignant fictions that disclose an adumbrated 'self,' otherness becomes the measure of life — the unexpected."

—Walter Abish

"Allen is also a visual artist of some renown, as one might guess from her painterly style, which delivers a slashing detail here, a dab of color there, and an economy of line that is frequently wondrous."

—Steve Almond

"Snapshots of the ineffable. Roberta Allen manages to tell with the language of subtlety the most poignant of stories."

—Luisa Valenzuela

"Roberta Allen writes like a latter-day Boccaccio."

—Library Journal

"Allen captures with magnificent nuance the emotions and moments that go with the territory of relating."

—The Brooklyn Rail

Contents

The Princess of Herself

The rude interruption of windswept snow rattling the windows reminds me that The Princess, the protagonist of the story I am going to write, is not on the island of Grenada, but sitting across the table from me at an upstate café. The café is surrounded by snow, so much snow I find it hard to focus at times on what she is telling me, the gist of which I will write as though I am hearing it for the first time while we lie on lounge chairs in front of a little bungalow like the one I rented seven years ago, shaded by fragrant nutmeg trees, little green lizards darting up and down the rough bark, gentle waves lapping the shore. It's easy to imagine the two of us in this setting.

The Princess, who receives monthly alimony and disability benefits and loves to travel (when her health allows) would seriously consider Grenada if I recommended it, especially if I told her how much I dislike Costa Rica where she is planning to go. 'Too many tourists,' I would say, 'and bad roads in the remote areas.' I can imagine her eyes, shiny like a doll's, glazing over, as she files the place "Grenada" away in a niche for future reference. Why Grenada? I wonder. Why not Vieques, for example, an island I know well? Or Belize? It isn't as though I had a great time in Grenada. Maybe Grenada came to mind because I've never written about it. Though it seemed to be the sort of place where something interesting might happen, nothing did, unless you count the night of my arrival when the female customs agent confiscated my expensive Clarins anti-aging cream. Did she *really* think I was hiding explosives in that brand new jar? I was furious enough to make a special trip—in vain!—to St. George, a capital I had no desire to visit, to see if I could find it in a pharmacy. I doubt I'll mention Grenada to The Princess. I'm sure she wouldn't like the interior which I experienced only once for a few hours with a guide who led me on treacherous trails through swampy rainforest. I had promised to send him a book I had written years ago about my trip to the Amazon but I never did. I think I blamed him for my being a klutz. He must have wondered how I'd managed in the Amazon.

But that's beside the point. In the café, I try to concentrate on The Princess who, unlike Victoria of Sweden or Astrid of Belgium, is only princess of a country I call *Herself*. Her interior is a mystery. This is why she interests me and why I am interested in the man I will call The Engineer. For ten months, he was closer to her than anyone else. I suppose I could also call him The Mathematician, for example, or even The Mechanic. But The Mechanic brings to mind Charles Bronson, tough and sexy in shoot 'em up movies (he must be very old or dead by now) and The Engineer isn't that type at all, just the opposite, in fact. Soft. I see him as soft. Like the little Pillsbury Doughboy on TV. I once ran into The Princess and The Engineer on the path around the reservoir. I was surprised to see him long-haired and bearded. Under his jacket I could tell that his belly was flatter. Love had transformed him. The Princess wore the wide white smile she always wears, which reminds me of the time a crown fell off her front tooth and The Engineer had to drop everything to drive her to the dentist. I can imagine The Princess in a bikini on the lounge chair in Grenada laughing about the crown that had caused her such distress.

Who is watching her laugh? The owner of that "Adventure Paradise" where I stayed perhaps? The divorced American expat desperate to find a wife to share his roomy turn-of-the-century plantation house? A lonely man whose efforts to entice a woman on match.com had failed (at least while I was there) though he told me he had offered free airfare to any female willing to meet him on the island. Would the American expat chase after The Princess, making a fool of himself? Would he be too eager to please, too "nice" in a phony kind of way? When he spoke, would his hot breath invade her personal space? He doesn't seem to know how to behave around women. I can see him running back and forth from the steamy kitchen in back of his outdoor restaurant on the bay, his bony chest exposed over baggy swimming trunks, his spindly legs seeming to fly in all directions.

"Get a move on, man, the lady is waiting!" he yells to the poor chef who is preparing a special dish for The Princess who can only eat certain foods. She is seated across from me at a vinyl-topped table.

Trying to calm him, The Princess says, "It's okay. I'm not in any hurry."

The Princess and I exchange looks that say, 'Who is this crazy man?' It's not difficult to imagine why the expat would be enamored with the youthful good looks of The Princess. Would anyone guess she's a grandmother? The Princess keeps that word at a distance the same way she keeps her son and daughter-in-law at a distance and the child who is her grandson. They are strangers, she tells me. The son she let her mother raise: "I wasn't meant to be a mother," she says, without regret. "I barely remember the partner I had then." I imagine her flicking her family from consciousness the way The Engineer might flick a mosquito. The Princess would *never* flick a mosquito in Grenada. She wears that easy 1960s go-with-the-flow smile except when she scrunches up her nose and shoos the annoying black flies from her face. Black flies are worse here than mosquitoes. Suddenly she points out the beautiful butterfly fluttering amidst the Heliconia. Beauty makes her shake her head in disbelief, in amazement even, though she has seen many butterflies on her travels and at home in the country. So has The Engineer. But The Engineer is not in Grenada. If he were, I would imagine him calling out excitedly, 'There's a Frampton's Flambeau,' or 'Look at that Antillean Cracker,' or 'See that Red Anartia?' I might even give him a butterfly net and let him catch a few, only to admire them, of course, before setting them free. I can easily imagine him following her to Grenada, afraid he will lose her which, of course, would be his fantasy, since he doesn't have her to begin with.

But that isn't the story I want to write. Maybe I should include The Senator I met in Grenada, who was not a senator but a toned and handsome, early-retired CEO; he was my idea of a senator, deeply tanned with prematurely white hair. He took me on a tour of his yacht and invited me to sail with him around the Caribbean. That trip would have made for a good story and is something I would have done, had I gone to Grenada when I was younger, although, after sailing around the Caribbean, I probably would have felt used or, for some other reason, sorry about accepting his invitation. Would The Princess be impressed by his yacht? While I try to imagine The Princess with The Senator, the howling wind and hurtling snow distract me, but not for long. I see her take The Senator's outstretched hand, a big hand that pulls her up from the inflatable dinghy to the yacht, moored offshore. The yacht is his baby. It's here that memory fails me. Did he say it was sixty-six feet long? The only word I am sure he said on my tour is "radar." I know so little about yachts I will either have to wing it or do research to make this scene plausible. I nod, smile, while The Princess continues talking. Have I missed something important? Something useful for this story? It's hardly the first time I've lost track of what she's saying. Am I giving too much importance to The Senator? She likes to flirt but she'd never go for him. He's too clean-cut. Too midwestern. And he was married, at least when I was there. Even if I imagine him divorced, unshaven, his hair long, she'd never go for his vote-for-me smile. He managed to sound dull even while telling me about the older couple he and his small crew rescued in a bad storm off the coast of Jamaica. But it might be interesting to have The Senator and the American expat pursue her. How would she react to their unwanted advances? What if The Engineer arrives later and rescues her? Would she appreciate him more? I look at her broad unlined forehead, the symmetrical features, the sallow skin, the mane of long gray curls falling past her shoulders, her shiny silver "moon" necklaces. Hippie necklaces. Behind her, the empty café. The polished wood tables. Downstairs, the ghost restaurant, noisy only in the tourist season when the main street is packed with people who ask, "Is this where *Woodstock* took place?" Up here, it's always quiet. I glance at two women hunched over laptops. The waitress leans on elbows behind the bar, as oblivious as The Princess is to the wind and snow whipping the windows.

"When I landed that morning in Albany, I felt sick," The Princess says, referring to a recent trip. "My stomach *really* hurt. I was in *no* condition to drive so I called and asked him to pick me up "

"Doesn't he work in Peekskill?" I ask.

"Yes," she says.

"Isn't Albany about a hundred miles away?"

She nods.

I look at her wide-eyed. *"You made him leave his office and drive a hundred miles to pick you up?"*

She nods again, as though I have no reason to be surprised. Maybe I don't. After all, *he* was the one, she told me last summer, who drove her to the emergency room more than once; *he* was the one who listened when she complained of unspecified aches and pains; *he* was the one who helped her through—what turned out to be—Lyme disease, then fibromyalgia and, not to forget, her chronic back "problems" that require weekly spinal injections. Have I mentioned that her medications often made her sicker than her illnesses? Have I said that she is allergic to everything?

But that is not all of her. There she is, shaking her head again and marveling at yet another butterfly or, this time, perhaps, a dragonfly. I know she likes dragonflies. Once The Princess wanted to show me the dead dragonfly she'd brought home. 'It's a good omen,' she had said. While she pauses to sip her latte in the café, I reflect a moment about *omens*. Didn't she tell me once she was a *wicca*? I try to remember. I'm listening to gusts of wind-blown snow outside when she says, "I knew from the moment we met that I would *never* fall in love with him. The spark wasn't there—you know what I mean. The spark I felt instantly with my ex-husband. But I loved talking to him."

The only time I fell ill on a trip was in Timbuktu where I had food poisoning from fish I had eaten the night before. But I won't go into that here. In Grenada I was fine. I am fine in the café sitting opposite The Princess though I am drinking too much coffee, which is probably why my stomach begins to ache, or am I reacting to her words when she says with a shrug, "I never considered what we had a *relationship*."

Unable to restrain myself, I lean in to the table and say in a voice louder than intended, "But you spent every weekend together!"

She smiles. An ineffable smile. What can I say to such a smile? She tosses the mane of long gray curls from her face. I understand (though The Princess doesn't) why she was asked—not politely—to leave the home of the woman friend she was visiting in Pittsburgh after saying about The Engineer, 'He never did anything for me.' While she speaks about this incident, I see her in Grenada, looking as innocent as she does now. Is she wondering how anyone could take offense at anything she's said or done? In her favor, at least she tried to discourage The Engineer from selling his house and buying a property only minutes away from her. When I look up in the café, I see the sun slowly sliding towards the horizon, obliterating the trees in front of it but not the snow, that heavy whiteness weighing down whatever it touches. Lying beside her on the lounge chair in Grenada, do I have the nerve to tell her she deserved her ex-husband? Did she deserve her ex-husband? A wealthy man, bearded and long-haired, whom I will call The Doctor. A man who suddenly left her, she says, for a younger woman after thirty-two years of marriage. For his pleasure, The Princess had engaged in sex with multiple partners, male and female, while he watched and sometimes joined in. "After all that openness," she says, "*he* had a clandestine relationship!" Her eyes open wide, her mouth tightens when she says the word *clandestine*. I imagine her saying the word *clandestine* in Grenada. Was she The Princess before he left her? Did he leave because she was The Princess? Or is The Princess the remains of the woman, the wife, the lover, who said about The Engineer after having sex with him once, "I just wasn't into him that way. It took me a couple of months to convince him that I only wanted his friendship." Perhaps at the moment she says this, a pelican or some other beautiful seabird swoops down into the water and disappears like the sun sinking in snow.

Ego Shrinker

At the bar I asked the architect to tell me about his dates with the beautiful blonde he called Body. What about her face? I wanted to say. Her surgically improved face was as beautiful as her personally trained body. Once, I asked why she told a friend that the Dutchman I am seeing was stalking her. "Has he followed you? Emailed you? Called you?"

Reflecting a moment, she said, "I guess it's

just me."

Why couldn't the architect be that honest?

Unlike Body, instead of answering my question, he only waved his arms in disgust, told bad Jewish jokes, and referred to Body as Ego Shrinker, which was not the same, he said, as Balls Buster. He refused to tell me what had happened between them unless I was willing to pay forty-two dollars for his dinner, plus tax and tip, and the dessert he suddenly decided to add to the bill.

Later, when she walked into the bar and greeted him, wearing a loose-fitting T-shirt instead of a little stretchy top, her hair pulled back tight in a ponytail instead of falling softly over her shoulders, she didn't look anything like herself, but that didn't stop the architect from complimenting her "swanlike" neck, to sweeten her perhaps, since he was, despite the failure of their recent romance, drawing up the plans for her new house.

Nonviolent Communication

The woman who treated me badly after her bout with breast cancer is trying to get back in my good graces by giving two poodle bookends to the toy poodle-owning ex-girlfriend of the Dutchman I am dating. The woman who beat the odds erroneously assumes that this ex-girlfriend is my close buddy because she is close to her husband's ex-girlfriend.

Her husband, an evil-looking elfin-like man, said to me at a party, giggling, and in his usual flirtatious manner, that all his life he has been good at getting his way.

Smiling, his wife explained to me that since she is back on Cymbalta, her antidepressant, she doesn't mind managing her husband's business though, of course, she would rather write like her sister who has published several books despite three bouts of breast cancer—not just one—and takes care of their aging mother who, the wife said, still smiling, will probably outlive them all.

Living on the Edge

In the country, the green-haired woman, drunk on gin and stoned on weed, drove over to my house from her own, a good half-hour away, and banged on the door to see if I, a woman who doesn't drive, wanted to go dancing at a club later on, since her phone, which she had balanced on the edge of the tub and forgotten, had fallen into the bath water as she orgasmed, having masturbated to a picture of a half-naked basketball star in *The New Yorker*.

This was probably not as crazy as my consenting to go out with her after cooking dinner for us both, though hours later, when even the band had stopped and it came time to go home, since she was drunker than ever and, having smoked more weed, glassy-eyed and swaying, I refused to drive with her. I chose instead to be driven by her married pal, whose husband was a stay-at-home type. She seemed slightly less inebriated and spacey. In the car, she proceeded to do Gurdjieff breathing exercises to "ground" herself, as she put it, before dropping me off on her way to another club where she and the green-haired woman would continue, she said with a wink, "living on the edge."

Barbeque

If I were to write a story about a barbeque in Stone Ridge, would I change the location to Willow? To Olive? Would I change the number of guests from six to five or maybe seven? Would I add another female? Would I exclude the odd-numbered male? Would I change the profession of the annoying architect swatting big fat flies at the table while we were eating to lawyer? Or pilot? Or yoga instructor? Did the architect swat flies *while* we were eating? Or was it later, after we had finished and taken the dishes and burnt buns back inside the house? Were the uneaten buns "burnt"? Or do I just like the sound of the words "burnt buns"? Did I say too much when I called the architect swatting flies "annoying"? Could I have said anything else? Could an architect be anything but annoying, slamming his big hairy hand on the table, squashing soft, gushy flies, or *almost* worse, missing them and cursing, causing us to pause in our conversation—about what? Cancer? Didn't the man I'll call, at least for the moment, the radio show personality, rather than the massage therapist I had thought of calling him because he is thin and wiry, which is how I imagine massage therapists, say that one out of every three people will get cancer at some point in their lives? Would I be giving too much away if I said that our host's cat likes to lick his bald head? If I said that two of the three male guests were bald and one wore a baseball cap and it was not the radio show personality, would you imagine I was talking about the annoying architect whose profession I have decided to change to lawyer because lawyers tend to be annoying, though not my present lawyer who amazes me with her attention to detail in regard to handling my insurance settlement which is probably irrelevant to the story. Would the baseball cap be superfluous? Clichéd? Should I leave it out, especially since a baseball cap reminds me of a day I spent in a motorboat on Lake Carefree with a man from Memphis I would rather forget? Should I reveal instead that one guest was missing a leg? And it wasn't the lawyer or the radio show personality? Should I say that I saw the prosthesis where his pant leg crept up ever so slightly as he laid his leg over the stool our host brought out from the house expressly for that purpose? Would the missing leg reveal his identity? Should I ruminate on the possible ways in which he might have lost it? Should I change his missing leg to a missing arm?

If I wrote a story about that afternoon, our sitting under the tall leafy trees around a table set down on the grass, the pool and decrepit bath house down a short hill, hidden by trees and shrubs, the unheated water still too cold in early summer for swimming, would that be painting too close a picture of the actual scene even if I didn't mention the big fat black-and-white cat with the bushy tail, the same cat who likes licking the bald man's head and is beloved by one of the women who brought an old reflex camera she is learning to use, to shoot pictures of the feline, whose name I have already forgotten? If I said that this woman didn't take any pictures after all, would that be giving away too much even if I didn't say that she hates her job or likes to sunbathe nude on the deck of her house where no one can see her? Would I give her a name? Cecile, for instance? Or Nicole? A name I love. Or would I simply refer to her as the reflex camera woman? And what about the wife of the one-legged man? And what about myself, the narrator? Would I say that I never asked the wife of the one-legged man whether they had any children, assuming, erroneously perhaps, that they had none because of her husband's disability?

What would I quote myself as saying besides, "How fortunate we are to be sitting here on a beautiful day like this," if indeed I said that while looking up at the blue sky between the tall trees whose name I don't know but would like to know almost enough to take out my cell even though I'm writing this on a bus to New York and the driver said a cell can be used only for emergencies. Still, I would like to call our host to find out exactly what kind of trees they are since I only remember the name "Ground Ivy" which our host used when bending down and tearing out a clump with his bare hand in response to something the wife of the one-legged man said. And what about our host? Should I mention that he once passed out from the smell of vinyl? That he said, "Shower curtains are the most dangerous." Should I add that by then I was only half-listening; that I, like the others, dozed off after drinking red wine and eating organic hamburgers despite the aggressive mosquitoes and gnats and, of course, the big black flies? Should I mention that our host also served potato salad and that the reflex camera woman brought a salad with cucumbers, tomatoes, and red onions, a salad she said her mother used to make? Should I mention that her mother lives in a nursing home like my own mother and that she is dissatisfied with her mother's care unlike another friend of mine whose mother has a twenty-four hour nurse and lives in her own apartment in Santa Barbara or should I say Phoenix? Would I be going too far afield to bring into the story people who weren't at the barbeque? The Dutchman, my boyfriend, for instance, who is thousands of miles away in Kyrgyzstan? Or the lawyer's lover or ex-lover—I'm not sure which—who last time I saw her seemed to be missing a tooth? Or our host's ex-girlfriend who swore the last time they broke up was really the end? Or should I, the narrator, mention my surprise upon hearing our host or was it the radio show personality or the lawyer, but certainly not the one-legged man, since his voice was too soft for me to hear anything, say that musicians in the subway audition for their spots, which led me to say excitedly, "What! In those dirty overcrowded stations?"

If I were to write this story, would I say

that while we were sitting there eating and drinking and talking about subway musicians and Ground Ivy and vinyl and shower curtains, death would soon take one of us? Would I wonder, as I often do when someone dies, why one person was chosen over another? Would I mention a terrible accident that happened on the highway near our host's house? Would I make that part of the story? Would I make it happen after the barbeque that night? Would I mention the starry sky? The sweet-smelling air? The sharp flashing lights in the distance? The soft white flowers on the catalpa trees in full bloom? Were they in full bloom then? The long line of cars, mine among them, waiting for the charred remains of the SUV to be cleared off the road? Would I mention the ambulance that left the scene empty? The helicopter airlifting the victim to a special burn unit perhaps? Which guest would be my victim? The reflex camera woman who let me drive home alone—which is illegal with only a learner's permit—from her house at the end of a dark dirt road, ditches on either side, at 2 am the night of the accident? For the sake of a story, could I kill off a close friend who made a bad decision? If I were heartless enough to make her the victim, would she recognize herself and never speak to me again? Should I kill off someone I like less? How about our host who gruffly asked me to *color* the black and white drawing I gave him in gratitude for taking me to the driving test I failed? Or the fly-swatting lawyer? Would any one of them not be angry or upset? Why should I worry about killing off one of my characters even if they do resemble people I know in real life? Why should I worry about anyone's *feelings*? Do any of them worry about mine?

Unfair to Apes

An animal named Jimmy called me on the phone screaming that I ordered a storm window for the closet. *I did not order a storm window*. I told him to get me a price on one that I would order only if it were cheap enough, since I could get the handyman who was anyway building me a shelf in the bedroom to just nail a board over the window so the cold air wouldn't blow in whenever I opened the closet door.

Whoever heard of a window in a closet?

But that's beside the point.

The point is that Jimmy acted like an animal and I feel badly about using the word "animal" because I wouldn't even know what kind of animal to say he was. I like a lot of animals but not the squirrel that tore apart my favorite succulent and for what?

Bugs to eat?

As I said, I feel badly about using the word "animal" in a context that is unfair to animals but Jimmy was wrong to scream at me the way he did for ordering something I never ordered. If he had been a little guy, perhaps him screaming at me wouldn't have been as horrifying as it was, but imagining this muscle-bound ape coming at me through the phone, as though he could squeeze his square body through the instrument, was even scarier to me than the night a year ago when I heard a terrific crash outside my house.

I imagined kids throwing rocks from a passing car or a big bird like a buzzard falling dead against my front door; imaginings that were less frightening than my discovery next morning that the large clay planters on my porch had been smashed by a black bear, an animal even stronger and scarier than Jimmy.

Suppose

Suppose you were sixty-one, had bought a car, had taken twenty lessons from the only certified instructor in Ulster County (a guy you called "The Thug," who loved talking about local gang shootings and his Brooklyn days boozing in bars), while you went through red lights and stop signs, endangering strangers and so-called friends like the one who said, "Maybe you're too uncoordinated to drive."

Or the green-haired woman who said, "Something is definitely wrong with you." Or the painter you were dating who blurted out, "Sell the car!"

Suppose that, in desperation, having failed three driving tests, you hired, to help you drive, an ex-social worker, still smarting from the "injustice" of being fired for breaking professional rules by taking into her home a Nigerian client. The Nigerian woman then betrayed her to her boss, depriving her not only of income for herself, her sickly father and her adopted Indonesian baby, but of the possibility of ever working again in her field.

Suppose that same ex-social worker forced you, while driving, to listen to her many complaints in the worst New York accent, not only about her job loss, but about her latest lover who'd left her, her failure to make friends since her move from the Bronx, her father's dependency, and, at forty-four, her many attempts at in vitro fertilization, using sperm from her Nepalese husband, who lives in another state and had married her to get a green card.

As a driving teacher she wasn't bad.

But when you complained about her habitual lateness, she accused you of being unprofessional and confusing business with friendship because you told her about your unfortunate affair with a man in Memphis.

Would you still hesitate to fire her?

Without her knowledge, you had hired a former ambulance driver with waist-long hair who gave massages to dogs for a living and refused to drive with you again because he claimed his back was "acting up." Then there was the terrified chauffeur who shrieked when you nearly backed into a trashcan, and insisted you see a mechanic because the sound of your engine convinced him that your poor old Cabriolet convertible was ready to explode.

Violence

I watched the retired internist who never
got over losing his beautiful, sweet, kind,
charming, funny, wonderful, perfect wife to
lung cancer, dive nude into the pool where,
at least for several minutes while doing a
masterful crawl, he could not make snide or
sarcastic remarks which, if you were female,
were all you ever heard, but, in his favor, I
can say that he took great care of his body,

working out in the gym, I was told, as well as skiing, which is why he actually looked sexy, making me forget for the moment or two that I was in heat, his violence when he swung me around on the dance floor, twisting, shoving, pulling me this way and that, hurting me to relieve his pain.

Killer

My car is a little animal. One of those fluffy little white lap dogs. A *Bichon Frise*. Friendly, gentle, cheerful, with spirally curls and sensitive skin. But I'm supposed to see it as a killer—a pit bull perhaps that tears people apart. At least "Killer" is what my good friend's husband calls my car. I call him "the hysterical man" when he sits in the passenger seat and I am the one behind the wheel. Maybe his faulty eyesight makes him see accidents where there are none and makes him sweat till the little car, sick from his stink, wants to explode, which is not far from how *I* feel when I smell his fear and his longish white hair flies even without wind, as if trying to take off and escape his malodorous scent. "Killer" is not his only word for my old white Cabriolet convertible. "This is a two-ton weapon!" he shouts. But, to me, it is still small and fluffy as it cradles me in its arms, licks my face with its warm pink tongue. I want to lose myself in its embrace, which may be the reason why the hysterical white-haired man is scared.

Need

At every party on Saturday night, the way she smiles, first at me, then at the Dutchman, you'd think we were lovebirds, a foot from the altar, honeymoon bound. I see that smile whenever she mentions him—which is often, especially when she's in the car driving me on errands. Over and over, I've told her and other party-goers in this artsy upstate town, that my rela-tionship with the Dutchman is noncommittal, but they just don't seem to get it. Whenever her white-haired husband sees me alone, he asks, "Where's your guy?"

I shrug and say, "I don't keep tabs on him."

I remind him that the Dutchman I am dating stays with me only three days a week. The other days he's at home in the city. I could be prowling the weekend flea market in town, walking down Main Street, or looking in the bookshop window, which I was doing this morning, when he asks me for the umpteenth time.

Later, I run into the green-haired woman in the local health food store. She says with a knowing smile, her voice full of innuendo, "How's your boyfriend?"

"Fine," I reply, my voice flat, as I recall her saying to him at a party: *I know you'd like to do me.*

These older, well-heeled partygoers, mostly from the city, smoke so much marijuana it must impair their thinking. Or else they're too old to remember open relationships, even though they once were hippies, like the aging, long-haired dropouts who congregate at the village square. Sleeping around is not something he and I do. In fact, we've been faithful ever since we met. At least, that's what we tell each other.

The wife of the white-haired man is unhappy, but she doesn't admit it. She and her husband still have sex once a month, she has said. I don't talk about my sex life. Nevertheless, she has often told me that regular sex has made my hair grow thicker. Once, I actually ran my fingers through my hair.

Why spoil her fantasies or the fantasies of other partygoers who spend time and energy wondering, or gossiping about, the sex they imagine other people are having, or not having, or about the sex they wish they were having, especially with the Dutchman. He is handsome and youthful despite his years. Who can blame them for flirting with him at Saturday night parties, given the scarcity of available older men without paunches draped over their pants and hairs sprouting like weeds from nostrils and ears. Like teenagers at synagogue dances, women dance with women at parties to Led Zeppelin, the Who, the Stones, and men stand on the sidelines and watch until booze, or pot, or both, give them courage enough to make their moves.

In summer, on Friday nights like this one, when local bands play '60s rock at a dance club in a nearby town, I miss the Dutchman. I grow tired of dancing with the same women, week after week, especially with the green-haired woman, who shimmies on all fours when she's drunk enough. After plenty of booze, partygoers repair to the club gazebo, outside in back, to smoke marijuana. I follow after them.

What else can I do?

I depend on the party crowd. They fill in for the wife of the white-haired man when she's too busy to drive me. Without them, I am stuck in town, watching petunias grow on my porch.

I pray that I pass my driving test soon!

The gazebo is clogged with smoke when the club owner's wife, a judge, walks by, and looks the other way. None of the partygoers who drive me home from weekend soirées, often drunk, or impaired by drugs, or both, have ever been fined, or prosecuted, or had a license suspended or revoked—as far as I know.

Seated across from me in the gazebo, the stoned neurologist from the Bronx, nick-named *The Receptacle* by those who follow her sexual escapades, stares at me with glazed eyes. "Whatsamatter you don' like me?" I recall how she tried to entice the Dutchman at a party by grinding the air in front of him, in time to the music, while he and I sat quietly talking. How annoyed he was by her interruption. She was too stoned to notice.

Driving me to the gym last week, the widow, desperate to find a husband, said, "I would never date a man as flirtatious as your guy." Why didn't I tell her his flirtations mean nothing?

The wife of the white-haired man has told me over and over how unhappy I was before I met the Dutchman.

Unhappy? I asked her, "Did you see something in me that made you say that? Something in my face? My voice? The way I carried myself?"

Her answer is always vague: "I could just tell."

Is it possible I *am* happier? Hasn't my relationship with the Dutchman made me less dependent on the party crowd? When he's here, he drives me in my Cabriolet convertible, the car I naively purchased before understanding how difficult driving would be for a woman my age I am almost ready to take my test again.

When I pass, will I still need the Dutchman?

Will the wife of the white-haired man still tell herself she is better off married when she sees me driving wherever I please? How much safer it is for her to complain about his short-term memory loss, and how she has to run his bed & breakfast, curb his spending on collectibles, handle investments, pay bills, do household chores, prepare meals, entertain his ex-wife and their married children and grandchildren, and even entertain an ex-girlfriend, besides hosting parties on weekends for the local crowd. Even her cancer didn't stop him from depending on her. "No time out for cancer!" was her frequent refrain.

Nevertheless, she recovered.

This last time the wife of the white-haired man went on about how unhappy I had been, I changed the subject by telling her about the kids who continued eating ice cream cones when their mother lost control of the car and crashed into a ditch, a story my driving teacher told me. I doubt she heard a word I said.

I've told her many times I don't want to be any man's wife, certainly not the Dutch-man's wife. He has never married; he has lived alone all his life. Every so often, he talks about wanting to fall madly in love, some-thing unknown to him. I hate to admit it, but sometimes I catch myself wishing we were Bill Holden and Jennifer Jones, picnicking under a large shade tree, in *Love Is A Many-Splendored Thing*.

Is there a picnic scene?

One night after a party, I was ready to call it quits. But he begged me not to end it. He had smoked pot like everyone else but me.

All evening he had chased a beautiful blonde realtor from room to room. Her disinterest made him more persistent. "You better watch that man!" drawled a pretty southern transplant. Later, she would leave her boyfriend because he'd flirted with the same blonde.

Raucous laughter in the gazebo doesn't stop me thinking about the blonde realtor. Maybe she changed her mind. Maybe she's entertaining him now in her Chelsea loft. Another blonde comes to mind, a famous female artist I ran into with the Dutchman in the city. After learning that he lived in Soho, the artist looked up at him with big blue eyes and innocently, or maybe not, asked if he ever visited me upstate. He said he'd stayed with me several times. I wanted to say that if several times meant three days a week for nearly six months, then several times was correct, but I let it slide, said nothing.

In the gazebo, I let the white-haired

husband interrupt my thoughts. In a loud, raspy voice, he is telling a story everyone but me is too stoned to remember hearing a thousand times before about a woman he dated forty-five years ago, who ended the relationship after telling him he would never make any money. "She's the one who spurred me on!" he says, laughing, phlegm catching in his throat. "She's the reason I became so successful. I found her on the Internet recently and told her so. But," he says, hysterical, barely able to get the words out, "she didn't remember who I was!" He doubles over in laughter. The others laugh hysterically too—except for his wife whose smile is pasted on her face.

This night is going to be a long one.

I glance at couples talking and drinking quietly at outdoor tables nearby.

Snakelike

The green-haired woman told me she had a cold in one nostril which she used as an excuse to break our date one evening when she must have found a party to go to with a friend more likely to get stoned than I and therefore more fun to be with, since she lived to have fun and get stoned.

She had no inhibitions about suddenly stripping off her bikini, meant for a female thirty years younger, at a party one afternoon and jumping into the hot tub with a flirtatious married man who was nude, and as stoned as she was, while his wife fumed even more than she had on the night of another party when the green-haired woman slithered over to her husband. He was, at least on that occasion, fully clothed and seated outside on a bench when she wound her body around him, snake-like, or as snakelike as she could get, which was *too* snakelike for his wife who shouted, "You're too close to him!" This didn't stop her husband from giggling, which made his wife even angrier and finally made the husband angry at his wife, which might have been some consolation to the green-haired woman who, it was said, was hit by a car when she was seven and had spent a year in a body brace, unable to move.

Forbidden Territory

If this ex-boyfriend—the one before the Dutchman—didn't mind my writing about his family or if I could disguise them in such a way that my ex-boyfriend wouldn't recognize his family, would I still want to write about them? Isn't at least part of my interest in writing about his family the fact that I promised *never* to do so? Is going back on my word a measure of my immaturity? Will reading this to him assuage any guilt I may feel?

I know it's possible for some writers to create characters purely from imagination, but it feels unnecessary to fill the world with more fictional characters when there are so many characters who are not fictional and should be written about exactly for that reason. Anything can be made up, but the things that happen in real life—for example, the invasion of toads in a Chinese village, right before the big earthquake, which, according to the inhabitants, was a sign of impending doom or the spontaneous fainting spells of *all* the girls in an Egyptian school, the cause of which has never been discovered—interest me precisely because these events are *real*. But this doesn't solve my quandary about writing about my ex-boyfriend's family which I, of course, could do under another name but that would be like turning the author into a fictional character— creating yet another fiction.

His fear, of course, is that I will say something derogatory, something he wouldn't want the world to know. Considering the number of readers who may stumble upon this story, however, using the phrase "the world," is laughable. But I think he knows me well enough to imagine that in a certain *smirky* kind of mood I might write something he won't like.

Before I met his parents, I had only met the parents of one other boyfriend who wasn't really a boyfriend but a man I hoped would be my boyfriend. I thought, erroneously, that because he'd invited me home for dinner to meet his parents I would soon get my wish. I was in Australia at the time. Later, I was informed that meeting his family was some sort of *Australian* thing.

I've never been big on "family" the way my ex-boyfriend is, calling his mother and sisters often and making frequent visits "home," especially now that his father is gone and his mother is alone in the house in the country. Will my ex mind if I say that I dreaded meeting his mother simply because *she was his mother*? I was pleasantly surprised, however, at how easy it was to talk to her, how she laughed a lot, giggled really, and made me feel right at home, which is something I never felt in my own family. Am I on the right trail? A trail my ex will approve? A trail away from forbidden territory. Away from barbed wire. Away from land mines.

What if I mention the cobwebs?

Will my ex take offense if I say that the first thing I noticed were cobwebs when I entered his parents' house? If I tell you how shocked I was by the cobwebs, will he say that cobwebs are no big deal? And isn't he right? After all, that room, though it was a *large* room (and would have been the living room in someone else's house), was only used for storing old discarded furniture and decades of dusty flea market finds. This reminded me (a little) of a man I knew, a Ph.D, who spent his entire two million dollar inheritance on board games (!) that he stacked to the ceiling in his Manhattan apartment, leaving him no space to live. He did not have cobwebs, however. At least, I don't recall any. I can feel *the daggers* aimed at me in the eyes of my ex at this point for mentioning, not only the cobwebs, but the clutter in the storage room which, in time, his mother sold in a series of yard sales. To be fair, I should say that several years after that first visit, I moved from the city to the country and now have cobwebs of my own. The other day, in fact, I watched a tiny spider trap a much larger ladybug while the spider dangled on a thread of light. Then, however, I couldn't stop thinking about the cobwebs (which were nowhere else in the house) while his mother kept talking, giggling, about something I don't remember. I only remember her smiling and friendly and nothing like the grim picture I had painted in my mind of a "mother." She said that once she had found a snake in the bathroom, as though it was perfectly natural to find a snake in the house.

Would I ever understand her? A mother wearing bermuda shorts, a T-shirt, hair cropped short, a mother who mowed the lawn and gardened and taught her son to play ball? A mother who wore sturdy shoes and hiked in the woods with her son and two daughters? A mother called Sally by her children?

How about a father they called Ben? Why was it easier to understand a father called Ben? A father asleep in an easy chair in the living room, which is the way I drew my own father once when I was twelve. Later, after my father's death, my mother and I found a fortune in change that must have fallen out of his pants' pockets over the years and lay buried until we looked under the cushion.

Ben's chair was beige. A beige naugahyde chair with wide arms that over time seemed to consume Ben, who had once been tall and husky. He seemed to slowly liquify into that slick plasticity. Is it wrong to say Ben was sick? Is sickness something to hide? Something to be ashamed of? Maybe I shouldn't have mentioned his illness before saying that I felt instantly connected to him, maybe because he and my ex looked so much alike, and although his father was nearly eighty, I found him as attractive as I found his son, maybe even more so.

Will my ex be shocked by this?

I liked the slow way his father spoke, carefully considering each word before it left his lips. Ben, who had been an architect, a *thinking* man, who also drew and painted. Ben, whose large sable brush I still use. By the time he was blind, had he forgotten or lost interest in dictating his life story into a tape recorder? A project I had encouraged him to start—while he still could. Music was Ben's last frontier. He played a recorder and sang old songs, accompanied by my ex on guitar. The whole family was musical. Sometimes they would sit in a circle, play instruments, and sing.

Now that I've said the word "family" again, can I include my ex-boyfriend's sisters without giving away family secrets? Can I say his father's illness was only one family tragedy? Doesn't every family have one or more tragedies? In the framed family portrait hanging in the hall, taken nearly thirty years ago and slightly faded by the sun, I think I see a hint of tragedy in their faces. Or is it only because *I know*?

Does a tragedy ever end?

Once my ex gave a ukulele to one of his sisters. But I no longer remember which one. Was it the sister who, every week, would sit for hours by the kitchen window, slowly, carefully copying with colored markers pictures from Sally's mail-order catalogs? Or the secretive one who lives up north in a subzero climate, who cuts her mother's hair when she comes to visit but lets her own hair grow waist long? For the sake of the story, have I said too little about his sisters? About the tragedy?

Or have I already revealed too much?

Am I bringing up past pain? Digging my finger in wounds that will never heal? Am I running the risk of damaging—or worse, ruining—my close friendship with my ex? Am I creating yet another tragedy? A tragedy I could easily avoid by respecting his wishes? Is *tragedy* too strong a word to use? Am I being melodramatic? Isn't tragedy the word we use for something that was *never* supposed to happen?

Something that divides life into *before* and *after*? When tragedy strikes, don't we still try to believe it didn't happen? Say it's a dream? A nightmare from which we will escape? When we don't escape, what then? What does my ex do? He plays guitar and sings in a group. He spends one evening a week at a chess club. He dates a poet in Astoria. He walks on a beach in Long Island. He drinks a little vodka before bed. He takes the sister who doesn't get out much to the mall. He helps his mother around the house. His mother prays, goes to church. It helps, she says.

Every Man's Nightmare

After listening to her obsess for an hour on my speaker phone, my ex-boyfriend called her "every man's nightmare." I don't remember exactly what she said, only her hysterical voice as she spoke about the man she'd gone out with the evening before, a man she *liked* who, in the moment of trying to kiss her goodnight, unleashed every demon she normally drowned in red wine, but, evidently, she hadn't had enough red wine to drink, or maybe there wasn't enough red wine in all the liquor stores combined in the county to drown the fear his attempted kiss let loose, which made her tell him, probably with the same breathless rush of words I was hearing on the phone, that another woman they both knew was much better suited to him than she would ever be, and that she'd be happy to give him her number since she was incapable of having an intimate relationship or, for that matter, a casual relationship with him or anyone else, so sure was she that she'd wind up ruining everything, which is exactly what she did, without even having, what could have been for someone else, the sweetness of a kiss.

The Man Who Carries The Dog

The green-haired woman, who is a kleptomaniac and was once jailed for fraud, calls the German woman's new boyfriend 'The Man Who Carries The Dog'. He usually walks a few paces behind his German girlfriend, carrying her miniature poodle in his arms. The poodle is female but has a masculine-sounding German name. German is her boyfriend's second language though I've never heard him speak

German. I've rarely heard him say anything—even in English. When I asked if he and his girlfriend had a good Christmas eve, however, he surprised me by saying, "Yes, but nothing I can speak about." This made me wonder if this seemingly meek, morose Irishman had a wild side he kept hidden, unlike the green-haired woman who hid nothing but the things she stole. I could easily imagine the uninhibited and lively green-haired woman having wild sex but it was hard to imagine the meek, morose Irishman having any sex, especially after he wound up in the hospital several times. The first time he had gallstones, then a bleeding pancreas and finally a mild heart attack. At that point, he seemed to give up hope. I found the kleptomania and jail time of the green-haired woman preferable to the sickness and depression of 'The Man Who Carries The Dog' though no one has asked me to choose.

Hot

He wants me to look hot. So I look hot. As hot as a sixty-year-old woman can look on Halloween without a bra. I'm jiggling under a shiny black teddy, trimmed with lace. Until I tried on the teddy in the thrift shop, I felt like those old women with long pancake breasts in ethnographic films, sitting in grass huts, kneading something doughlike.

In my short butt-hugging, stomach-crunching black skirt—another thrift store bargain—I feel squirmy, wormlike, narrow enough to inch through tight spaces like the thought, 'Why am I doing this?' which sneaks through my self-admiration.

I had trouble pulling up the black tights so there wouldn't be space between the crotch of my tights and that of my panties which someone might see when I sit. On my feet, black boots with heels, of course. Pointy-toed would've been better than round-toed but the thrift store didn't have my size.

I always scoffed at Halloween even at ten, trick-or-treating with kids on 63rd Drive in Queens. Once a voice said *Nobody's home!* when we knocked. But this Halloween is different. Up here, they make a fuss, squeeze as much fun as they can out of it. I'm all for fun. At least I'm trying to be, though I'm not sure about my date. He was dead serious when he told me to look hot. He called me three times in two days to discuss my costume.

"How about a bikini?" he asked.

"I don't have one. How about my Chinese bathrobe?"

"What would you be in a Chinese bathrobe?"

"What would I be in a bikini?"

"Hot! You'd be hot. Is the Chinese bathrobe hot?"

"No. Not really. I have a sarong from Bali."

"Is it hot?"

I picture myself in Bali, sarong tied at the waist, T-shirt on top, rubber sandals on my feet. "No."

"Don't you have something low-cut? Something sexy? Something tight?"

It's a big deal party he's taking me to.

When he picks me up on Halloween night and takes off his coat, he wears a Japanese robe with Japanese letters on the back, over a T-shirt and exercise pants. I wonder who or what he's supposed to be. But I don't ask. I figure he was too involved in my outfit to give much thought to his own.

He spins me around. "You look really hot! I didn't know you had such a hot body! You always wear things that hide it!"

From the back, he cups my breasts. "Sorry," he says, when I give him a look. We're not up to that. He's still trying to get over his former lover. But from the moment when he told me to look hot, I've been hoping tonight would be the night. He doesn't know I got this body late. It comes from the gym and the pool and the track. But I never thought to show it off before, especially my knees, which have always been fat. But he says my knees look fine.

When we started dating a few weeks ago, I told Sarah I didn't like his sloping shoulders and kinky hair and large pores or acne scars or both. But I got over that. What I can't get over is the way he suddenly folds up inside like some mutant origami. The worst night was his birthday when he took me to the blues club where his former lover belts out ballads. That night someone else sang.

Lights from the party in the large house, high on the mountain, sneak through the dark woods as he stops the Ford van behind a slew of parked cars. When we get out, he says, "That's *her* Toyota!"

"Did you know she'd be here?"

"No!"

Thoughts are running through me like cockroaches. The big black shiny kind. *Is he just using me to make her jealous? To get her back?* It's a long walk from the car to the house. I try to shoo the cockroaches.

The door is open. Our host, whose height would make him a spectacle on any night other than Halloween, yells out hello. He wears a monk's robe. A small Asian employee takes our coats. The crowd at the bar doesn't notice our entrance. They'd be a nameless bunch to me even if they weren't in costume. I'm new around here and know few people besides my date.

In the large living room, I see eyes. A roomful of eyes. Eyes behind masks. Eyes behind feathers. Eyes of devils, monsters, goblins, werewolves, ghosts. Eyes of a Suzanne Somers look-alike. Stoned eyes. Roving eyes. Downcast eyes. Glassy eyes. Sneaky eyes. Animal eyes. Eyes framed by screaming red wigs, blonde wigs, black wigs, green wigs, witches' hats. Then bodies. One in a skin-tight leotard. One in a floor-length gown. Several in sparkly tops. One Hansel and one Gretel. One Humpty Dumpty. Two in tuxedos. One in diapers. A pony-tailed flasher in a pinwheel hat with a big open coat. Bodies with hairy arms, hairy legs. Bodies draped in loose fabrics, off-the-shoulder sheets.

Which of those eyes, those bodies, belong to *her*? My arms press firmly against my sides. Suddenly they feel fat. The rest of me feels fat too even though Ken and Steven and Larry, my date's friends, lean in and kiss me, say I look hot. I feel eyes on me. Men's eyes. Women's eyes. I sit down on a loveseat. Lou licks his lips. I don't count Carl, the crasher. Chest hairs stick out of Carl's low-cut print dress, long blond hairs from his wig tickle my shoulder when he kisses my neck, tells me how hot I look.

I am the only French whore. My date brings me vodka. As I take a sip, I see the smile—*her* smile. Before he says a word, I know it's her. Elaine. I recognize three moles in a row down her right cheek though I've never seen her before and didn't know she had any moles. She smiles at me, then pulls him close, kisses him.

"On the lips!" he says, angrily. "For God's

sakes, why'd you kiss me on the lips?"

Something wakes up in him. It's not the anger. The anger is always awake. What wakes up behind the anger is hurt. The hurt is green. It writhes and twists like the tail of an alligator caught in a vice.

Elaine doesn't have a body like yours, he had said in my house. She's hidden from neck to knees in something loose and white, her hair hidden under a wig. A wig like one I should've bought to hide my hair. Bad hair. Thin. Not French whore hair. Wet dog hair. Hair isn't the issue, however.

A man in street clothes brushes my date's shoulder, smirks. Did he buy that nose in a store? Is his mouth real? As real as mouths behind masks, talking, eating, drinking, laughing? I hear him murmur, "Thanks for the job, pal." My date looks angry, murmurs something back.

In my partially inebriated state, I look

at the man in street clothes and decide that people are more real when they are *truly* fake. I imagine this thought as wisdom.

"That's Elaine's date!" he says to me. "A plumber! *I* hired *him* to fix Elaine's sink! Did you hear him *thanking* me?"

What pushes me into the next moment? Even when I don't want to go. While he elbows me from bar to buffet, he mutters, "That bastard! Thanking me! Thanking me for introducing them!" I remember when Elaine left his slippers and his neatly folded robe on his doormat. *Does that mean she wants me back?* he said. We eat slabs of smoked salmon, drink more vodka, talk to guests with voices that come from somewhere else. Switzerland? Rome? Atlantis? Mars? Hell?

I smile, laugh, shake my head, nod, look surprised, look amused. I hear words leave my mouth. Do I know what I'm saying? What they're saying? Have I a clue? Are clinking glasses clues? Who is talking to me behind a black mask? If I dig my finger deep into the fabric of his costume, will my finger hit fat? Muscle? Bone? Nothing? Are we in a movie? Who is "we"?

Elaine and her date leave early. They're *going* to bed! my date's eyes say. I understand those words. Unspoken.

Talking to monsters, devils, witches, the Suzanne Somers look-alike, the diapered man, the flasher, soon seems ordinary. "There's no music! We need music!" my date says suddenly to our host. Even our needs seem ordinary. As ordinary as looking hot. As ordinary as sleeping alone.

You Look Like Fun

Why she, the green-haired woman, let herself be seduced by the tall, lean, handsome musician/truck driver, is easy to imagine, even after he told her he had gone crazy one night many years ago on his motorcycle and spent two years in jail, where he stopped drinking and got his life together.

Driving his truck, playing local gigs and raising two daughters alone—from two different women—daughters he hadn't initially wanted but grew to love, kept him busy, especially caring for the "little one," a six-year-old who screamed, "Daddy! Daddy! Daddy! Watch me!" as she doggie-paddled in the backyard pool while he phoned the green-haired woman. He had met her a few nights earlier at the large outdoor birthday party where he played guitar with his band. On his break, he had said to her, "You look like fun."

When she saw him again, he spoke reverently about a pink-haired woman he had known some time ago. That woman had meant something to him but evidently the green-haired woman did not, since he chose never to call her again after they had sex. Having told her before they got into bed that he hadn't had sex for two years, never calling her again wasn't half as bad as him saying, just before he orgasmed, "So this is what a woman feels like," which made the green-haired woman feel less womanly than almost anything else he could have said.

Eight-Inch Heels

"She's suing me for two million," the retired CEO says to the other guests, still seated at the table after a huge turkey dinner in the loft-like space of an old but renovated hunter's cabin, bordering a state park, deep in the woods.

"Oh, that's ridiculous!" says the big-boned Finnish blonde who was recently arrested for DWI and told the officer he'd be perfect in Iraq when he refused to open the hand-cuffs cutting her wrists. Her nostrils flare as she says in her heavy accent, "Did you see the heels she had on that night?"

"Eight inches!" says the neurologist. Her accent says Bronx. The neurologist is known for her voracious sexual appetite. "She had on eight-inch heels."

"Are there shoes with eight-inch heels?" the writer asks. She believes she is better than the company she keeps. No one answers. Maybe no one hears. Maybe they are too caught up in the singer's lawsuit. The writer glances at the hostess, busy at the work station in the open kitchen.

"I took her to the hospital that night after she fell. It cost me $5,000! She didn't have any insurance," he says. He pours Remy into a glass and gulps it down. The writer wonders if anyone else notices hair growing on his bald scalp.

Seated beside him, a woman with a knack for invisibility, offers him her empty glass. "I love Remy," she says, in her invisible voice. When she speaks, her words don't belong to her. They hang anonymously in the air.

The neurologist and the teacher with a raspy voice, say in unison, "Remy is the best."

"Now she claims she can't play the piano!" the retired CEO says, filling the invisible woman's glass. No one has noticed how much wine she's had this evening or, for that matter, on any other evening.

The neurologist says, "Didn't she just have a gig in Seattle?"

The writer wonders why no one mentions the black ice in his driveway the night the singer fell. Given his wealth, she wonders why he didn't have the ice cleared before the party. After all, he has a live-in housekeeper and cook on his estate. She, too, would have fallen had she not grabbed the arm of the painter, seated directly across from her, stoned and silent, a badge with the old Rolling Stones tongue logo pinned on his pink shirt. The painter looks disdainfully at the other guests as he pours more Johnny Walker Black.

"I thought she just had a gig in Seattle," the neurologist says again, too high to know she's repeating herself. She smiles mischievously which is the way she smiles when driving her 2004 Ferrari. She drives so fast even the Finnish woman refuses to ride with her.

The painter stares at the neurologist and mutters, loud enough for the writer to hear, "She's so masculine! So aggressive!"

"Of course she broke bones falling on that ice. She's so skinny!" the Finnish woman says about the singer.

"But she's beautiful and she looks so young," the writer says, dreamily, envy in her voice, as she recalls the skimpy, spangled, spaghetti-strapped mini-dress the singer wore that night and how she and the painter danced cheek-to-cheek as though they were lovers.

"No," the retired CEO says, shaking his head vehemently. "She's not beautiful and she looks her age. Sixty-five!"

The teacher with a recent nose job, her brain burned out from heavy drinking and snorting cocaine in her youth, stands up and says, "Stop it! I'm her friend. I don't want to hear you all talking behind her back! I can only imagine what you say about me."

The teacher claimed she had her nose done because of a deviated septum. The hook never bothered her, she said. The writer was surprised that most people didn't notice she'd had her nose done at all.

"She's my friend too!" the Finnish woman says. "But she's anorexic. She said to me, 'I weigh ninety-eight pounds. I feel so fat.' She's 5'8", for god's sake!"

The teacher sits down.

"She's anorexic?" says the writer, incredulous. "No! I don't believe that." While waiting for dessert, a chocolate mousse cheesecake and a scrumptious—at least to her—blackberry pie, she takes another Ghirardelli Pure Dark Chocolate from the candy dish full of truffles and Godiva to-die-for delectables.

The teacher who worries about her weight watches her. The teacher had one glass of wine. After Hepatitis B, this is her limit. She's trying to save what's left of her liver.

Nodding to the writer, the Finnish woman says, "Yes! She's anorexic." The Finnish woman drinks wine and eats nothing but chocolates. She had her Thanksgiving dinner at noon. Her son made her cook turkey. Her thirty-five year-old son.

"She won't get two million," says the neurologist who closes her country house in winter because she can't drive fast in snow.

"I have a $550,000 insurance policy. She

can't get more than that," he says, looking worried despite the joints he'd smoked, the wine and Remy he'd imbibed. Whether he has taken Ecstasy yet is a matter for conjecture.

The writer likes to see him smile—which he hasn't done since mentioning the singer's lawsuit. When he smiles, he reminds her of the Cheshire cat in *Alice in Wonderland*. That smile with perfect white teeth. Too perfect. Too white.

As the hostess bends over the sink, washing dishes, the writer wonders if her blue eyes are always glazed. Nights when she's out partying and getting stoned, the hostess knows better than to try and drive to her secluded home and stays with friends instead. "I can't hear anything with the water running," she yells, anxious when she's not at the center of things. She probably thinks she's missing something important.

Finished with the dishes, she approaches

the table and asks, "Where's the pot? The big plastic bag full of pot." The guests look at each other, puzzled. "I saw it on the living room table before we sat down to eat," she says.

The woman with a knack for invisibility suddenly rises and rushes into the living room. Frantic, she searches every table, every shelf, looks under cushions on the couch, behind the bookcase, the DVD player, the TV, beneath the chairs from Kenya. "Not here!" she calls out, her voice, for once, her own.

"Didn't you have it?" they turn and ask each other. They shake their heads no. "Then who has it?" they ask, squirming, beginning to panic. Only the writer, who doesn't do drugs, realizes that they've already smoked it. But she says nothing. She picks up another Ghirardelli Pure Dark Chocolate and pops it into her mouth.

The Opening

At the gallery in Chelsea I saw a woman on video shave her pubic hair and, later, walk naked through Venice, but it turns out that I missed the best part of another performance piece in which an artist, who slowly releases a raw egg from her vagina, throws it at the screen where it smashes—as though in the face of the viewer—and runs down the glass looking like cum. I only saw the part where she lifts her pink sheath, exposing herself and then the egg, when he, who had planted a fallen branch with his bare hands in my front yard in the country and crowned it with a rusting fleur-de-lis he bought for $3 at a tag sale, establishing himself as king of my domain, walked into the opening and barely acknowledged me because, he said later, we had talked on our cells minutes earlier, which, in his mind, gave him reason to deny my existence, making me mad enough to miss not only the egg smashing on screen but another more famous artist pulling out a scroll from her projected wall-size vagina, and, in a black and white video, a naked fat woman bouncing around on the floor.

Normal

The two nude men in the pool with their flabby muscles and shriveled dicks are not a pretty sight, especially the older one who has mental problems and was told by the green-haired woman, a few minutes before he disrobed, that he should live in a nursing home because his house is a pigsty and he can't take care of himself. This didn't faze him, however, because he doesn't hear anyone but himself.

Being intelligent, he tends to fool people into thinking he is normal if they don't speak to him for more than a few minutes, after which time they realize he is pontificating about this or that or quoting long obscure poems that interest no one, not even the other nude man in the pool, who feels empathetic towards him and tries to help him by befriending him, or so he imagines, denying to himself that life alone in the country with a dog blinded by a porcupine can be lonely and dull for a retiree if he doesn't dredge up characters who are easy to find in this town but—what he doesn't know yet—are hard to lose once he's found them.

Easter Sunday

I didn't write about the night the Dutchman, my new ex, made me nervous enough in my Cabriolet to turn left without looking to my right, when a car zoomed toward us, missing us by a hair. Or the time he grabbed the wheel on Route 28 and drove into oncoming traffic. I didn't write about those incidents here because they didn't happen on Easter Sunday, the day of our visit to Valatie.

My story, which isn't finished yet, is based on fact, as is the case with many of my stories. However, quite a few details are fictional. The Dutchman has always recognized himself in my stories. But he is the sort of man who would recognize himself in a story even if the character *wasn't* based on him. His criticism often angered me. He complained that I didn't stick to *facts* even though I told him over and over that I consider my stories *fiction.* Still, he contradicted me with comments like: *It didn't happen like that!* Or: *I didn't say that! You're putting words in my mouth!* Or: *Why don't you write about the good times?*

Fortunately I won't have to listen to his comments about this story. I can write freely about the screaming match on the way to Valatie and about our Easter Sunday luncheon at the cottage of our host and his partner. I can exaggerate as much as I want, make him a monster if I feel like it.

The argument on the way to Valatie stands out as being the worst screaming match we'd ever had. It lasted two and a half hours with only a couple of brief breaks. Of course if he had read this, he would've contradicted me and said: *It took less than two hours!* I kept mispronouncing Valatie while we screamed at each other on the road. Correcting me over and over, he said, "It's pronounced 'va LAY sha,' *not* VAL-a-TIE!" The village was named by the Dutch for the little falls, 'vaaltje,' that dominate its center, which our hosts made a point of showing us when we *finally* arrived.

Why I was invited was a mystery until our host told me his partner loved my novel and wanted to meet me. The Dutchman, who I was seeing then, had never met them before.

When I broke up with the Dutchman, I said, "You think the world revolves around you!" Had he read those words, he would've said, *Why did you write that?* I would've said,

Because it's true! He would have replied, *You never said that! And I don't remember you breaking up with me.* I'm sure he'd believe that. He hears only what he wants to hear. Did he only pay attention to me in bed or when I was driving or when he was reading my fiction? Despite him yelling at me, I could tell he liked being a character in my stories—no matter how I portrayed him—it proved to him that I cared. Or so he thought.

Our host, who once wore a ponytail like the Dutchman, was younger than the Dutchman and me by more than a decade. I could say he was an old friend, but he wasn't. He was an abstract painter whose ex-wife had once been my close friend. He invited me a couple of weeks after we bumped into each other in the city. I hadn't seen him for several years.

Though her smiles tried to hide it, I could tell that his partner, in face and figure a younger version of his ex-wife, was as bothered as he was by our lateness. "How could it take you so long to get here?" the painter asked us, incredulous, while his partner, a writer like myself, reheated some fancy dish that was not supposed to be reheated. It was Easter Sunday, as I have mentioned, with dyed eggs—lavender and blue—and bottles of good wine. "It shouldn't have taken more than forty-five minutes at most," our host said, his face flushed or maybe it was sunburnt, I couldn't tell which. His hair, shorter than I'd ever seen it, was slicked straight back.

Wine made me honest so I told them we'd had a huge fight and gotten lost, but our host and his partner continued to look at us in disbelief. Our fight started, I told them—as though details would help them understand— when I turned on Ms. Garnier, which is the name I gave my GPS. Naming her made her feel more like a friend. Like a friend, Ms. Garnier is not always right. Once when I was driving to a party—held by a sculptor with the name of an Egyptian goddess—Ms. Garnier announced that I had arrived while I was making a hairpin turn but there wasn't a building in sight. Recently she had failed to find a party in a converted church on Route 28.

If he had been reading this story, I could not have written that Ms. Garnier had failed me twice. Making Ms. Garnier wrong was the same thing as making *me* wrong. Since Ms. Garnier guided me to the right destinations, I couldn't understand why he always disputed her directions, finding what he called *better* routes on a map. At one point while he and Ms. Garnier competed for my attention, I became so confused I shrieked, "Stop telling me how to drive!" Then I *froze* on 9N. Or was it 9S? Or 9W?

I toned down our shrieking and my confusion when informing our host and his partner about the details of our argument. What would they have thought if they'd known how vindictive we had been? What would they have said? Or done? I imagine them at the table, squirming in their seats, too embarrassed to even look at us. But I'm unsure how the Dutchman would have responded. What would he have said—if anything? Would he have zoned out? I've seen that glassy-eyed look on his face before. Would he have misunderstood what I was saying? His English wasn't always as good as he thought. Would he have felt shy? Sometimes he was shy with strangers.

I had to admit that sometimes in the car I felt hazy, unfocused. *Dreamy* says it best. But I was better behind the wheel when he was *not* in the car. Learning to drive and finally passing my test at my advanced age was no small feat. Responding to this he would have said, accusingly, *Why haven't you written that I helped you learn how to drive?* I would've said,

Because you act as though I still don't know how!
There wasn't any test to prepare me for his
nearly nonstop orders on the road. I'd been
befuddled enough to ask on the way to Valatie,
"Is that left?" while looking at a left-pointing
arrow. In disbelief, he had said, "What are
you—three years old?"

Often his directions were wrong, though
not in the case of Valatie. As it turned out,
Ms. Garnier, which I had switched off then
on again in protest, eventually directed us to
Main Street—but in the wrong village. Still,
his being right did not justify him screaming
at me, "Why didn't you turn? Didn't you see
the sign?" I exploded, "Shut up! Shut up!
Shut up! I can't stand you screaming at me
anymore!"

My sudden and extreme outburst reminds
me of the "Fuck you!" he shouted once in
terror when I'd come close, months earlier,
to colliding with a car in the next lane on

the New Jersey Turnpike. I can imagine how happy he would've been to read that—but he might have been dozing by then. He'd often dozed while reading my stories—but not for long. At least while he was dozing he couldn't criticize what I had written. I would not have minded him dozing through the next part. There isn't a pleasant way to write that often he got so angry or excited or upset I didn't understand his directions because his words became a mishmash of English and Dutch. If he had read that, he would've yelled, *You make me sound like an idiot!* I would've said, *I'm just writing the truth!*

Having toned down or left out the most dramatic parts of our argument, I must have bored our host and his partner. They finally stopped me by showing us around their cottage. I had called the cottage adorable, because it was, especially the kitchen, which was roomy enough for the table where we were eating. The cottage even had a washer and dryer.

The washer and dryer remind me that I have to get to the laundry before it closes. If I didn't have to leave now, would I try to find an insightful way to end this story? A surprising way?

Almost a week has passed since our trip on Easter Sunday. After I drop off the laundry, will I be able to admit that the Dutchman and I enjoyed ourselves in Valatie?

Or instead of continuing my story, will I turn my attention to the tall pines, the maples, the cloudless sky, and go to the swimming hole? After all, it is very hot and still too soon to remember the good times, especially since this is Friday, the day he usually took the earliest bus from the city and, while I slept, let himself in with the key he would take from the mailbox beside the door.

The Unwashed Glass

I wanted to jog around the lake again, breathe in the fragrant ferns, gaze at the blue-gray mountains, the leafy maples and pines edging the shore. Instead, since *she* had the car and said she had jogged enough for one day, I went with her to the house of a woman she had recently met, a woman I didn't want to know, who invited us out on the porch, where we sat in front of a garden with huge blue and purple hydrangeas while she told me with a pseudo British accent that she worked in publishing, and I drank from a tall glass what I thought was only spring water even though it had a strange smell and taste. It dawned on me as the two women discussed renovations on their houses, that the substance not washed out of the glass before the woman poured water in it was scotch. For the woman to have given me an unwashed glass was, to my way of thinking, either careless or insulting, but no more careless or insulting than the treatment I had received at the hands of the friend who had brought me to her house. I wondered if this woman in publishing, on whose deck we were sitting, knew, through some sort of mental telepathy, to treat me as badly or as thoughtlessly as the one who *claimed* to be my *good* friend, and had made at least one reference to being just that before proceeding to do things even my own mother wouldn't have done, in the days when my mother, who has since lost her edge to old age, treated me as badly as she did.

Forgotten

When one of the stars of *Sex and the City* bumped into me in the health food store on Sixth Avenue, I remembered Katherine saying, "I wish I had close female friends like the girls in *Sex and the City*." That trivial incident set my mind in motion. I couldn't remember Katherine without remembering Valerie and Yolanda too. I squint, as though squinting can help me remember.

Why do I want to remember?

Is it possible to have feelings for people I've more or less forgotten?

Or is it fear that drives me?

Fear that my memory is failing.

I try to imagine Katherine's face, but all I see is a blur. Only her short dark curly hair is clear. We had the same hair stylist who had once fallen twenty feet off a cliff while hiking. She landed on her feet. Doctors said she would never walk again.

I remember that hair stylist telling me about a man who threw a live mouse into burning leaf litter in his yard and how the blazing creature ran out and through the front door, setting his house on fire. She said the house burned down.

When did I last think of that?

I try harder to picture Katherine the night she made that remark about *Sex and the City.* I see us seated side by side at a table in a pricey restaurant. This seems odd to me now. I suppose we both wanted to face the large windows and look out at the night and Highway 212, quiet at that hour. I see her sipping from *my* glass of Merlot.

Why?

Was she cheap?

Poor?

Thrifty?

Was I annoyed?

I must have been annoyed.

I remember thinking how young she looked even though she was retired and collecting Social Security. I was surprised a woman her age would be hooked on *Sex and the City.* Social Security seemed far in the future then. It wasn't that far.

If I asked, would she remember making

that remark?

Who can tell what will be remembered?

Is it true that with each telling, our memories change?

Without electronic devices, who can prove what anyone has said?

Even when we hear the same words, those words say something different to each of us.

What something means can change from one moment to the next.

What does it mean to remember four baby robins dead in the nest under the eaves of my cottage? Would I remember the baby birds and their mother who never returned if the friend who found them did not often remind me?

How many of our memories are fabrications?

Distortions?

Having said that, can I be certain that anything I say is true?

Was Katherine the loner I remember?

Until her comment about *Sex and the City*, I thought she was fiercely independent. She spent her time protesting for peace and driving as far as Vermont just to tango.

Despite her busyness, she had time to watch every episode of *Sex and the City*. So did I. There was little to do in our village. This is probably why I recall running into her at some event at Town Hall I no longer remember. I had gone there with Valerie. When I introduced them, I didn't think they would click.

I'm almost sure *Sex and the City* was not mentioned then but I can easily imagine Valerie, who was younger than us and only watched old movies on TV, scrunching up her face and saying, 'How can you watch that show!'

When the event at Town Hall was over, the three of us were approached by Yolanda, a woman about Katherine's age who was new to the village. She invited us back to her house for a drink. Her boldness impressed me.

As I recall, her house was nearby. In the living room or maybe it was the dining room, I worried that her husband, stooped and frail, might collapse from the effort of opening the wine as I watched him walk off and close the door behind him so he wouldn't disturb us. Yolanda's eyes followed him too.

I remember thinking that Yolanda must have been a beauty in her youth before she gained weight.

What made me think so?

Her fine features?

A framed photo?

Or did I just make that up?

When I imagine that late afternoon, it feels dreamlike: our mad laughter, our joyful shrieks (about what I no longer recall), even Katherine's excited voice saying, "This is great!

Let's get together for Sunday brunch every two weeks!"

Were these her exact words?

Where do words go once they leave our lips?

Do they dissolve in the air?

Or is there a giant repository with all the words that were ever spoken?

If so, how would we find which ones were ours?

Maybe in that giant repository, the words would belong to us all—even words we wish we'd never said, never heard.

How many words have I forgotten?

I don't remember what Valerie said when she offered to host our first brunch. I only recall my surprise. Valerie was cool about most things. I saw her more than most people did but that was not often.

Her demanding job required her to be on

the road before dawn four days a week. Two out of three days off, she spent at the nursing home where her mother cried and pleaded with her to stay at the end of each visit.

No wonder she hit the vodka.

Valerie used Absolut to make Bloody Marys at our Sunday brunch. Funny—I remember that, but I've forgotten whether the brunch took place in summer or winter, spring or fall.

What I remember well is the abstract painting Valerie hated that hung on the wall in her mudroom. She had tried to return the painting after buying it on a whim but the artist refused to take it back.

I am tempted to say Valerie wore a sour expression whenever she laid eyes on it.

Maybe she did.

Every object but that painting in her spare and tasteful house had been chosen and placed with the utmost care. Of course, I don't recall every object but saying this feels true.

Is *feeling* enough to make it true?

I want to say her house was as clean as it was neat. When Katherine walked in that Sunday and looked around, I am almost sure she said to Valerie, "God, this place is clean enough to eat off the floor!"

Was she bothered by what I think was Valerie's obsession with cleanliness and order?

I try to picture Katherine's house. I wonder now, as I may have done then, what her house was like. I want to say her rooms were messy, clothes and flyers strewn about, cat hairs on the couch, plants crying out for water—

Can the *desire* to remember fool you into believing that you do?

In Valerie's spacious sun-soaked living room, the Cyclamen by the window provided the only splash of color and seem as real to me now as the jade plants lining the sill in my studio. But I can't remember whether the

Cyclamen were hot pink or fuchsia.

Looking back, I wonder how Valerie could have been depressed in a room so bright.

Did I wonder about that at the brunch?

I remember more about that Sunday afternoon than I do about that late morning when we all arrived. I have completely forgotten Yolanda's arrival.

I wish I could recall how the brunch began as vividly as I recall Valerie's hand-washed underwear drying on the rack upstairs in the middle of a room that may have been the attic, with a washing machine and dryer, a room so filled with sunlight I could feel the presence of God or Spirit or whatever, until she said, "Everything dries in an hour."

Thinking about that now, I doubt she would have shown a room with drying under-wear to people she didn't know well.

But her immaculate white bedroom was

another story. How clearly I see that room.

White down comforter.

White dresser.

White chair.

White night table.

White lamps.

White curtains.

Did she show us around the house before we sat down to eat?

Or did I see the bedroom on another visit?

I picture the kitchen: long, narrow, spotless. Not even a hint that she'd prepared a meal for four. I can imagine Katherine saying in a critical way, "Not a crumb in sight."

I never remember food so I am not surprised I have forgotten what Valerie served that day.

I have even forgotten the name of the dish my Venezuelan friend ordered last week when we lunched at a Vietnamese restaurant on

Canal Street though I wanted to remember so I could order it myself sometime. I only know my Venezuelan friend's entrée consisted of various kinds of fish and was cooked at the table. The steam made me sweat.

I am tempted to say Valerie did not sweat— even on hot summer days. When she wasn't working or seeing her mother or cajoled into attending a weekend party with the usual crowd, I imagine her in the bedroom upstairs, reading by the air-conditioner—also white.

Did Valerie's hands tremble slightly as she placed what I guess were eggs or omelets on the round oak table? Was that the only sign that something was amiss in her psyche?

At best, a fuzzy image of us seated around the table floats before me.

Then nothing.

Nothing.

The sort of *nothing* that brings to mind the blackness of huge Australian caves, the floors of which suddenly drop to infinite depths, or so it seems, at least in memory.

What is the difference between memory and imagination?

Is there a difference?

Can we remember without imagining?

I see us all after brunch, bellies full, heads a bit woozy, lounging in the living room on the large overstuffed couch and easy chairs.

Is this a memory?

I assume alcohol had loosened our lips. Conversation must have turned to men. Why else would I recall Katherine saying that men were suddenly paying attention to her again. Surprising me, she said, "I thought that part of my life was over."

I remember those words as clearly as I recall the man with a Rapunzel-like ponytail with whom she later had a relationship.

A man Valerie would have snubbed.

Valerie didn't have a boyfriend. She liked to be alone or so she said. I picture her tall slender figure moving silently from the kitchen to the living room, holding yet another open bottle of Merlot. The "heart throb" of several local men she had spurned, I imagine Valerie listening to us carefully while refilling each one's glass as well as her own, keeping to herself stories she had told me when she was drunk one night about her annulled marriage to a "boring psychologist."

At the time of that brunch, was I still dating the artist who bar mitzvahed his collie, then thirteen, in front of twenty-five guests on the lawn of his property? A former girlfriend had given him the collie ten years earlier. She still called to ask after the animal. I remember him saying, "I feel like she and I were married and had a dog."

When Yolanda met me on the street with

him, she had whispered in my ear, "He's a catch!"

I have said little about Yolanda who owned several properties with her husband in the Dominican Republic and worried about their upkeep. She lived upstate intermittently.

Not long after we met, I recall her saying, "I don't belong here." I tried to reassure her. I did not know what she was getting at until she said some time later, "This town is racist!" I disagreed until I realized the only other dark-skinned person I knew was the mathematician who dated a former beauty queen, a pale blue-eyed blonde from Alabama.

I began to wonder if Yolanda was right.

Maybe Yolanda, not Valerie, was the quiet one at that brunch, at least until her outburst. While the four of us relaxed around the large low coffee table in Valerie's living room,

Yolanda blurted, "I haven't had sex for a year!"

Her words hung in the air with the heaviness of wet laundry.

I was going to say that embarrassment left us speechless.

But now I wonder if we were merely surprised.

Whatever effect her words had, however, I doubt Yolanda noticed. I see her leaning forward in the easy chair, hands clenched, as she rushed on after taking a deep breath, "I have to have sex! I can't stand it, I'm so horny! My husband can't do it. He's too old. But he understands. He doesn't mind if I take a lover. He wants me to be happy."

I wish I could remember what we said in response but I feel as though I am standing before those black Australian caves again. I could easily slip off the edge.

If I said she asked us to introduce her to some available men, would I be making that up?

What does my forgetfulness mean?

I only recall that we agreed to meet again two weeks later for Sunday brunch at Katherine's house.

In anticipation of our second brunch, I bought Benadryl a few days later to avoid having an allergic reaction to Katherine's two short-haired cats even though Valerie had whispered to me, as I was leaving her spotless house, that she now knew way more than she wanted to about Yolanda, and that night phoned to say, "Katherine stayed and stayed! I thought she'd never go home!"

I recall how Katherine often kept me on the phone, talking politics, long after I said I had to get off.

The Friday evening following our Sunday get-together, Valerie refused to go with Yolanda and myself to the club where a local band played *The Rolling Stones*. I held my breath every time Yolanda asked a man to dance. When each one turned her down, she wore a brave face.

I felt bad for her, but not half as bad as I felt for the friend battling cancer and the one in the city fighting eviction from her Soho loft, neither of whom I had mentioned to Valerie, Katherine or Yolanda.

Whatever else transpired between the four of us in the days and weeks after our brunch, not to mention the next year, maybe two, is lost in those black Australian caves or dim at best except for the tiff I vaguely recall with Katherine.

Her neighbor was not supposed to know that she had been snooping around his house while he was away. I don't remember how he found out but Katherine blamed me. That ended our friendship. In retrospect, our friendship seemed fraught from the start.

After the brunch, Valerie and I must have had some good times but I only recall her saying, "I feel like staying home" or "I'm too tired" except when I suggested going out for a drink.

The last time I saw her was the day I invited friends over to say goodbye while I was packing. I still remember finding the unused Benadryl when I emptied the contents of the medicine cabinet into a carton.

Was I sad then?

Did I feel anything?

One night at a crowded downtown party in the city, a few years later, I was surprised to see Yolanda. She was still heavy but she looked elegant and at least ten years younger. A face-lift I presumed. I wondered if her husband was still living and whether she had found a lover. But we didn't even say hello.

ACKNOWLEDGMENTS

The following stories have appeared, some in different form, in journals and anthologies:

751 Magazine: "Ego Shrinker," "Snakelike"
Big Bridge: "Unfair to Apes," "Living on the Edge"
Bomb: "The Unwashed Glass"
Chronogram: "Killer"
Conjunctions: "Need"
Ducts: "Nonviolent Communication"
Flash Fire 500: "The Man Who Carries The Dog"
Flash: The International Short Story Magazine: "Ego Shrinker"
Gargoyle: "Normal"
Harp & Altar: "Forbidden Territory"
Mr. Beller's Neighborhood: "The Opening"
New Ohio Review: "Barbeque"
Salt River Review: "Suppose," "Every Man's Nightmare"
The Brooklyn Rail: "Hot," "Eight-Inch Heels"

The Collagist: "The Princess of Herself," "Forgotten," "Easter Sunday"

The Vestal Review: "Violence"

"Forbidden Territory" also appeared in the anthology *Harp & Altar, Writing from the first six issues,* (ed. Keith Newton and Eugene Lim, Ellipsis Press, Jackson Heights, New York, 2010)

"Hot" also appeared in the anthology *The Unbearables Big Book of Sex*, (ed. Ron Kolm + others, Autonomedia, Brooklyn, NY, 2011)

"Every Man's Nightmare" also appeared in *"In Like Company: Salt River Review & Porch Anthology* (ed. James Cervantes, Salt River Review, 2015)

"Forgotten," Honorable Mention, 2015 Gertrude Stein Award

ABOUT THE AUTHOR

Roberta Allen is the author of nine books, including three collections of short fiction, *The Traveling Woman* (Vehicle Editions), *Certain People* (Coffee House Press) and *The Princess of Herself* (Pelekinesis); a novella in short short stories, *The Daughter* (Autonomedia); a memoir, *Amazon Dream* (City Lights); the novel *The Dreaming Girl* (Painted Leaf 2000, Ellipsis Press 2011); and several writing guides. Allen was on the faculty of The New School for many years and has also taught at Columbia University. She was a Tennessee Williams Fellow in Fiction and a Yaddo Fellow. Her conceptual art, exhibited internationally, is held in the collection of The Metropolitan Museum of Art.